The book contains 4 tasks:

1. find the difference

2. count the hearts

3. color the picture

4. tell which way the vehicle is going, right or left?

Happy Valentine's Day and good luck!

THiS VALENTINE'S BOOK

belongs to

♥•♥•♥•♥•♥•♥•♥•♥•♥•♥•♥•♥•♥

KISS ME

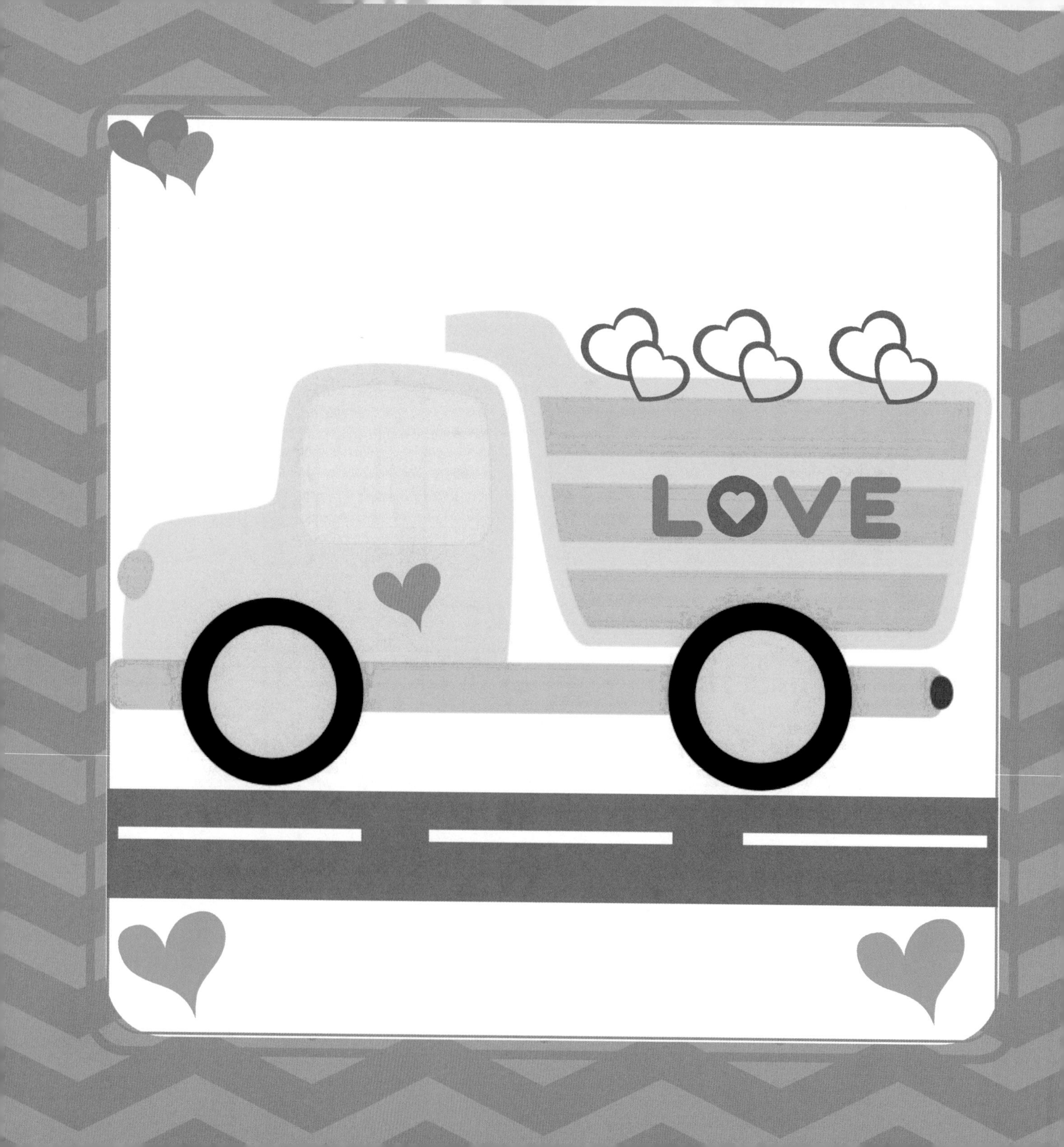
LOVE

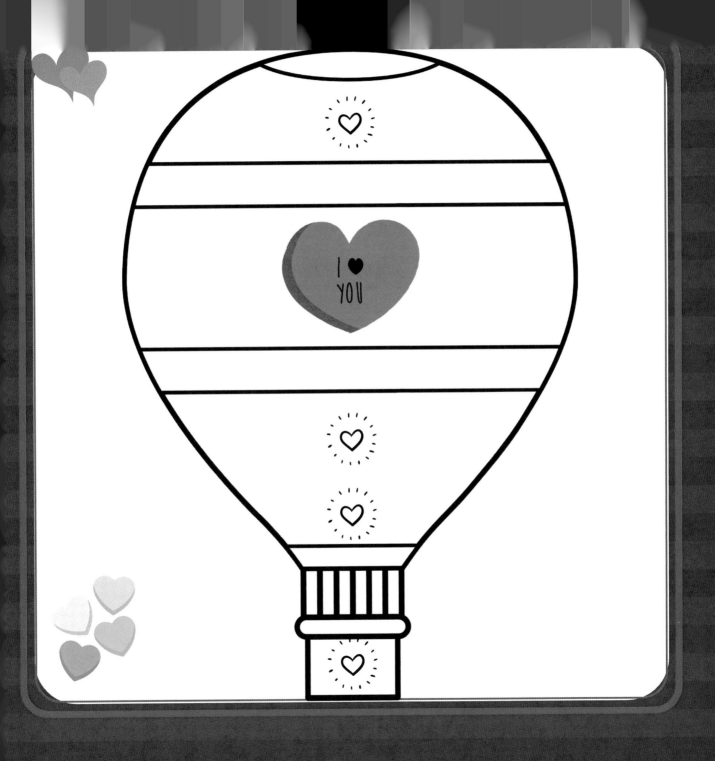

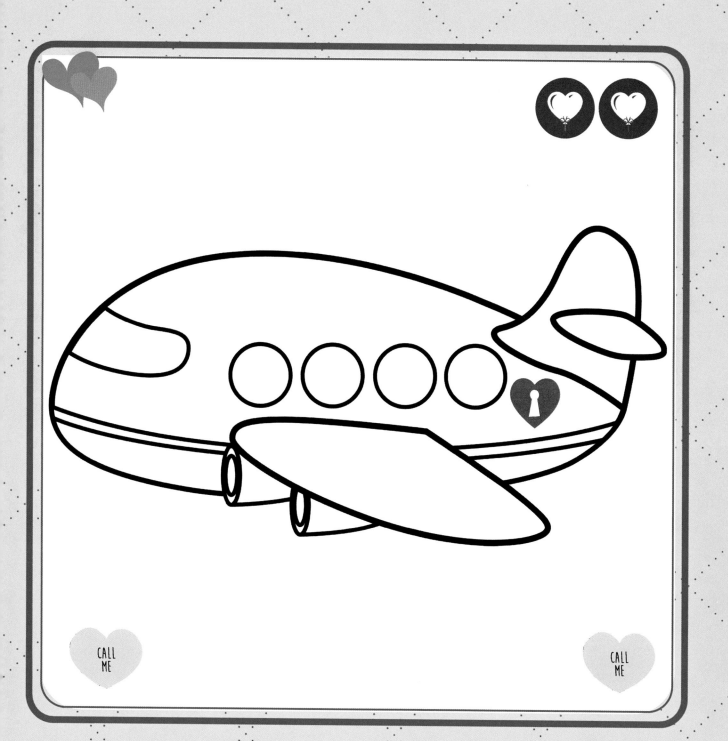

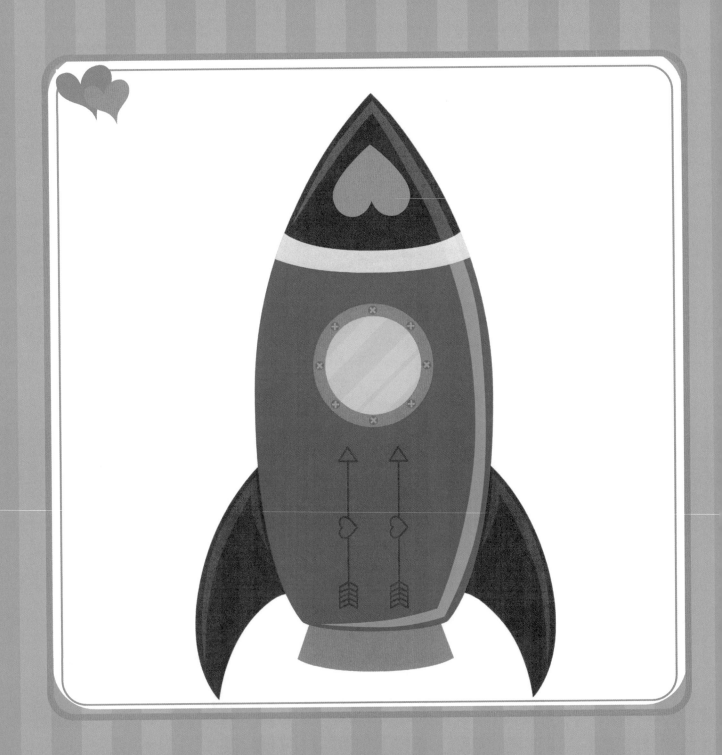

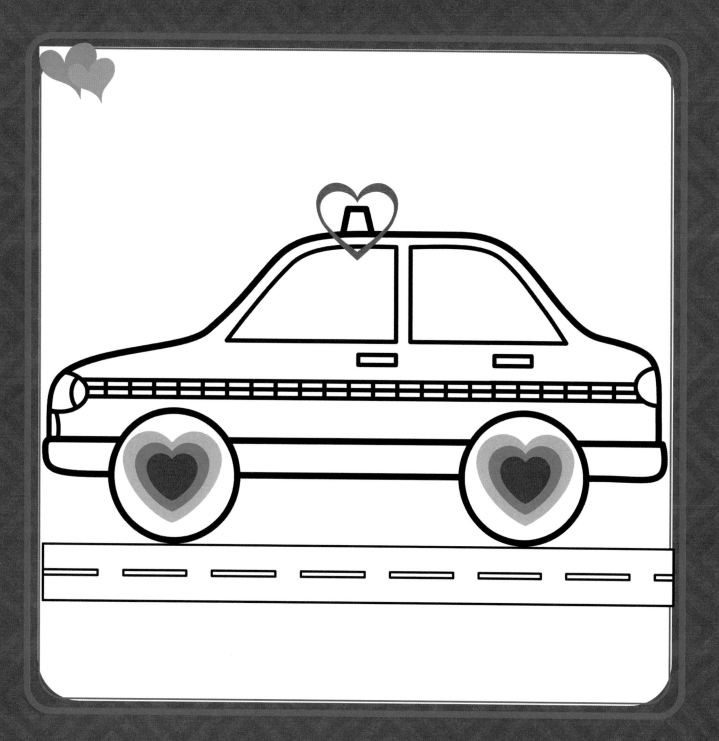

Made in the USA
Middletown, DE
05 February 2021

33154052R00024